Rotter and Rascal

For Mrs Marvellous

Other books by Paul Geraghty:

Dinosaur in Danger
Tortuga
Slobcat (mini treasure)
Solo

ROTTEN AND RASCAL
A RED FOX BOOK 978 0 099 43866 3

First published in Great Britain by Hutchinson,
an imprint of Random House Children's Books

Hutchinson edition published 2006
Red Fox edition published 2007

3 5 7 9 10 8 6 4 2

Copyright © Paul Geraghty, 2006

The right of Paul Geraghty to be identified as the author and illustrator
of this work has been asserted in accordance with the Copyright,
Designs and Patents Act 1988.

Red Fox Books are published by Random House Children's Books,
61–63 Uxbridge Road, London W5 5SA,
a division of The Random House Group Ltd,
London, Sydney, Auckland, Johannesburg, New Delhi and agencies throughout the world.

THE RANDOM HOUSE GROUP Limited Reg. No. 954009

www.kidsatrandomhouse.co.uk

A CIP catalogue record for this book is available from the British Library.

Printed in Singapore

Rotten and Rascal

The Two Terrible Pterosaur Twins

PAUL GERAGHTY

RED FOX

65 million years ago the world was a deafening place.

There were thunderstorms.

There were volcanoes.

There were landslides.

And there were earthquakes.

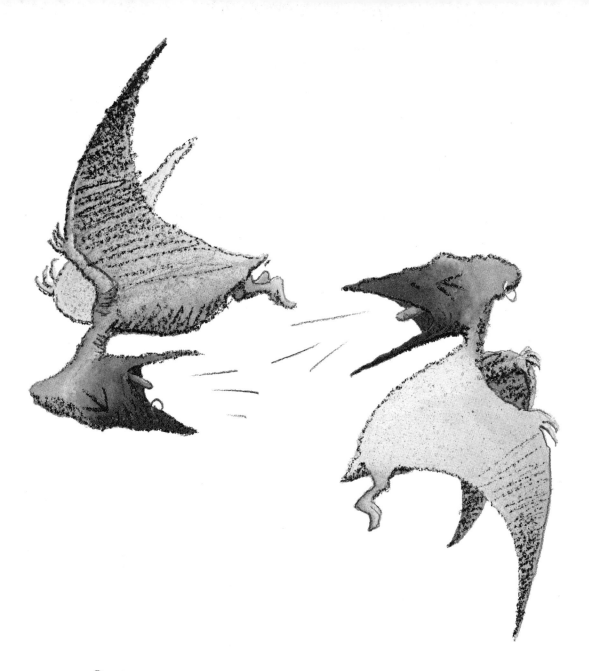

But most of the noise came from
Rotten and **Rascal,**
two terrible pterosaur twins.
By day they would yell at each other,
by night they would shout.

Come morning they'd be *screeching*,
by lunch they'd be **screaming** and
before bed they'd be **bellowing** again.

They just never stopped.

On Tuesday, Rotten saw a fish.

'It's **mine!**' yelled Rascal and they both dived down.

'I saw it **first**!' shouted Rotten.

'I saw it **loudest**!' bellowed Rascal.

'It's **mine!**' screeched Rotten.

'No it's not,' screamed Rascal. 'It's **mine!**'

'It's **mine!**'

'It's **mine!**'

And there was a hullabaloo . . .

. . . until Slim sidled up and said, 'You gotta have a good beak, brother. The fish should go to the one with the best beak.'

'No it's not,' shrieked Rotten. 'The fish is mine!'

'It's mine!' 'It's mine!'

And there was a horrible hullabaloo . . .

... until Violet veered into view and said,
'Hey, man, cool down. The fish should go to the one
with the best crest.'

'My crest's **brightest!**'
cried Rotten.

'My crest's **biggest!**'
howled Rascal.

'It's **mine!**'
'It's **mine!**'

And there was a
horrible heated hullabaloo . . .

. . . until Slippery swam up and said,
'It's simple: the best swimmer should get the fish.'
'I swim fastest!' shouted Rotten.
'I dive deepest!' shrieked Rascal.
'No you don't!' screamed Rotten. 'The fish is **mine!**'

'It's mine!'
'It's mine!'

And there was a horrible heated hullabaloo and a hubbub . . .

. . . until Clever concocted a cunning conclusion.
'The fish should go to the one who argues the least.'

'I argue **less**,' claimed Rotten.

'I argue the **least**,' argued Rascal.

'No you don't,' screamed Rotten. 'The fish is **mine**!'

'It's **mine**!'   'It's **mine**!'

And there was a horrible heated
hullabaloo and a howling hubbub . . .

... until Buster burst in and bellowed, 'What's the problem? The fish should go to the toughest pterosaur.'

'I'm **toughest!**' yelled Rotten.
'Can't be,' howled Rascal,
''cause I'm **tougher!**'

'Oh yeah?'
'Try me!'

So they kicked and fought till they both fell
to the floor, too tired to talk.

For a wonderful moment there was silence.

'I won,' Rotten panted at last.
'I won,' huffed Rascal.
'No you didn't. I won!'
'No you didn't. I won!'
And there was a horrible hysterical heated
hullabaloo and a howling hubbub . . .

. . . until Rex roared, 'HEY! Cut the scrapping and yelling. Which one of you is the fattest, the juiciest, the crunchiest and the tastiest?'

'I'm fattest!' yelled Rotten.

'I'm juiciest!' shouted Rascal.

'I'm the crunchiest!' bellowed Rotten.

'I'm the tastiest!' screamed Rascal . . .

. . . then they saw the gleam in Rex's eye.

Two terrified pterosaur twins tongue-tied in a
tyrannosaurus-shaped shadow finally stopped fighting.

But it was too late . . .

And just in case you were wondering,
they both tasted exactly the same.